Melissa's Octopus and other Unsuitable Pets

CHARLOTTE VOAKE

WALKER BOOKS
AND SUBSIDIARIES
ON · BOSTON · SYDNEY · AUCKLAND

Here is Melissa's octopus.

What a splendid creature he is.

Unfortunately, an octopus is not a very suitable pet.

You should see the mess he makes in the bathroom!

Thomas has a much
smaller pet –
a lovely little mole.
But the mole is always
digging tunnels,
which makes him
very hard to find.

Thomas never knows
where he'll pop up next.

Poor Betty!

She can never find her pet either.

He's a chameleon.

Where can he be today?

This is Arthur's warthog.

Isn't he a beautiful animal!

But a warthog is not a great pet.
A warthog does exactly what it wants.

Caroline's giraffe is a gentle pet
with lovely long legs.

But she's a bit too tall for Caroline.

This is Simon's worm.

He's not a bad pet, but Simon never knows which end to talk to.

This is Peter's elephant.
He is very big.

He is also VERY heavy.

Sometimes he's upstairs…

and he ends up downstairs by mistake.

Kevin and Bertrand
are very proud of their new pet crocodile.
They have invited Melissa, Thomas, Betty, Arthur,
Caroline, Simon and Peter round to see it.

Look at its glittering teeth!

And where are Melissa, Thomas, Betty, Arthur, Caroline, Simon and Peter?

Phew!

They're all having tea together.

But next time they'd
better watch out...

A crocodile really is ...

the MOST UNSUITABLE
PET OF ALL!

To my
beautiful
badly~behaved
pet parrot
Gwen

First published 2014 by Walker Books Ltd 87 Vauxhall Walk, London SE11 5HJ • This edition published 2015
2 4 6 8 10 9 7 5 3 1 • © 2014 Charlotte Voake • The right of Charlotte Voake to be identified
as author/illustrator of this work has been asserted by her in accordance with the Copyright,
Designs and Patents Act 1988 • This book has been typeset in Gill Sans Light • Printed in China
 British Library Cataloguing in Publication
Data: a catalogue record for this book is available from the British Library ISBN 978-1-4063-6100-1 • www.walker.co.uk